AR Quiz # 28221

BL: 3.1

Pts: 0.5

ARTHUR'S
FUNNY MONEY

ARTHUR'S
FUNNY MONEY

LILLIAN HOBAN

An I CAN READ Book®

Harper & Row, Publishers

I Can Read Book is a registered trademark of
Harper & Row, Publishers, Inc.

Library of Congress Cataloging in Publication Data
Hoban, Lillian.
    Arthur's funny money.

    (An I can read book)
    Summary: When Violet has a numbers problem and
Arthur is penniless, they go into business and solve
both problems.
    [1. Business enterprises—Fiction.
2. Chimpanzees—Fiction.] I. Title. II. Series: I
can read book.
PZ7.H635Arf 1981   [E]   80-7903
ISBN 0-06-022343-X   AACR2
ISBN 0-06-022344-8 (lib. bdg.)

To Ann Franklin,
Best of friends

It was Saturday morning.

Violet was counting numbers
on her fingers.

Arthur was counting the money
in his piggy bank.

He counted three dollars
and seventy-eight cents.

"Arthur," said Violet,

"do you know numbers?"

"Yes I do," said Arthur.

"I am working with numbers
right now."

"Well," said Violet,
"if I have five peas
and you take three
and give me back two,
how many peas will I have?"

"All of them," said Arthur.

"I don't like peas,

so I wouldn't take any."

"I know you don't like peas,"

said Violet. "But I am trying

to do a number problem.

Will you help me?"

"I have my own number problem,"

said Arthur.

He turned his piggy bank

upside down and shook it.

But no more money came out.

"I don't have five dollars

to buy a T-shirt

and matching cap," said Arthur.

"Everyone on our Frisbee team

has to buy them.

They have FAR OUT FRISBEES

printed on them in blue,

and they light up in the dark."

"Wilma's big sister

is running errands to make money,"

said Violet.

"She wants to buy

a new catcher's mitt."

"I don't like running errands,"

said Arthur.

"You could wash cars," said Violet.

"The junior high kids

always wash cars to raise money.

That's what they are doing

this afternoon."

"Well, if they are washing cars,
then I can't," said Arthur.
"There would be too many of us
in the car-wash business."

"I know!" said Violet.

"You could wash bikes!

Lots of kids would pay

to have their bikes washed."

"Great!" said Arthur.

"I could get the rust

off the wheels,

and I could shine up the frames.

I could make lots of money."

14

"That's no fair," said Violet.

"I told you about the bike wash.

But you never told me about the peas."

"I will," said Arthur.

"But first help me set up business."

Violet went into the kitchen.

She got a pail and a brush.

She got a cloth and a sponge.

Then she took them to the back steps.

Arthur was making a sign.

It said:

"There is no soap or Brillo,"
said Violet.

"We have to buy some."

Arthur put his money in a bag
and they went to the store.

Arthur bought a box of soap for 53¢
and a box of Brillo for 27¢.
"I hope lots of kids
want their bikes washed,"
said Violet.

When they got home,

Norman was waiting

with his little brother

and their dog, Bubbles.

"How much is it for a tricycle?"

asked Norman's little brother.

"The same as for a bike," said Arthur.

"But a trike is only
half as big as a bike,"
said Norman.

"You should charge half as much."

"Well," said Arthur,

"it's half as big,

but it has more wheels.

"Tell you what," said Norman.

"I will give you 38¢

for my bike and his trike.

How's that for a deal?"

Arthur thought about it.

He opened the box of soap.

He filled the pail with water.

Then he counted on his fingers

and thought some more.

23

"Look what Bubbles is doing,"
said Norman's little brother.

Bubbles was eating the soap
out of the box.

And he was drinking water
out of the pail.

"That's why we call him Bubbles,"
said Norman.

"He ate most of my soap,"
yelled Arthur.

"You better pay me back."

"I will give you 42¢

for washing the bike and the trike,"

said Norman quickly.

"You'll be able to buy

lots more soap."

"I don't want to buy more soap,"

said Arthur. "I want to buy

a Frisbee T-shirt and matching cap."

"Bubbles is eating Brillo

for dessert," said Violet.

"Get that dog out of here!"

shouted Arthur.

"He's spoiling my business!"

"You have to advertise

if you want business,"

said Norman.

"Tell you what I'll do for you . . .

you wash my bike and put a

sign on it saying:

ARTHUR WASHED ME

I'll ride all over town

and get you lots of business."

"Me too," said Norman's brother.

"It won't cost you anything,"

said Norman,

"and you'll make lots of money."

So Arthur washed

the bike and the trike.

He got the rust off the wheels.

And he shined up the frames.

Then he made two signs,

and put one on each of them.

"Okay," said Norman,

"we're ready to ride."

He gave Arthur 42¢

and he and his little brother

rode off.

Arthur put the 42¢ in the bag
with the rest of his money.
"You hold the money for me,"
he said to Violet, "and write down
every time I get some.
When it gets to $5.25,
I'm quitting."

"What's the extra 25¢ for?"

asked Violet.

"For licorice twists," said Arthur.

"I just love licorice twists."

He gave Violet some paper

and a pencil.

"Now," said Arthur, "write down $3.78.

That's how much I had to start.

Under that write

take away 53¢,

and take away 27¢.

That's for the soap and Brillo."

Violet wrote down all the numbers.

"Now add on 42¢," said Arthur.

"And that's how much I have now."

"How much is that?" asked Violet.

"Let's see," said Arthur,

and he started to count

on his fingers.

"I thought you said

you knew numbers," said Violet.

"I do," said Arthur. "Look!
There's a parade at the corner,
and it's coming this way!"
"That's not a parade," said Violet.
"It's Wilma and her cousin Peter
and his friend John."

Wilma was wheeling a doll buggy

with a rocking horse in it,

and she was pulling a stroller.

Peter was driving a fire engine

and pulling a wagon

with a sled in it.

John was riding a scooter
and carrying a skateboard.

"We saw the sign," said Wilma,
"and we came to get washed."

"Arthur only washes bikes,"
said Violet.

"No I don't," said Arthur quickly,

and he rolled up his sleeves.

He put more water in the pail,

and he put in the rest of the soap.

"Wow!" said Arthur.

"I'm going to clean up!

This will make me lots of money!"

Violet got her pencil and paper ready.

Wilma's cousin Peter

was whispering

something to Wilma.

"Wait a minute," said Wilma.

"We thought you washed for free."

"For free!" yelled Arthur.

"Can't you read that sign?"

Wilma's cousin whispered to her again.

"The sign on Norman's bike

didn't say anything about money,"

said Wilma.

"It's against the law

to tell a lie on a sign."

"I didn't tell a lie on a sign,"
said Arthur.

"This sign right here says
bikes washed 25¢.

And that's what I'm washing.

No scooters or doll buggies

or anything else!"

Arthur pulled his sleeves down.

Peter pulled Wilma's sleeve
and whispered some more.
"Okay," said Wilma.
"We'll go get our bikes.
You can wash them for 25¢ apiece
if you do the rest for free."

Arthur thought about it.

He looked at the empty box of soap.

He stirred the water in the pail.

"Tell you what," said Arthur.

"Throw in a little extra

so I can buy more soap,

and I will do it.

How's that for a deal?"

So Wilma and Peter and John
got their bikes.
Arthur scrubbed the wheels
and he shined the frames.
He washed the buggy, the stroller,
and the rocking horse for Wilma.
She gave Arthur 34¢.
He washed the fire engine, the sled,
and the wagon for Peter.
He gave Arthur 36¢.
He washed the scooter and the
skateboard for John.
He gave Arthur 33¢.

Violet put all the money in the bag,
and she wrote down all the numbers.

After Wilma and Peter and John left,

Arthur said,

"Now let's get more soap

so I can make more money."

Arthur and Violet

took the bag of money

and went to the store.

Arthur got a box of soap

and counted out 53¢.

"Sorry, son," said the grocer.

"This soap costs 64¢."

"But it was 53¢ this morning,"
said Arthur.

"That's right," said the grocer,
"but the price went up.
You can't get soap
at this morning's price
this afternoon."

"That's no fair," said Arthur.
"Maybe they still have it
at this morning's price
at some other store,"
said Violet.

Arthur and Violet

went down the street.

They passed the hardware store

and the fruit-and-vegetable store.

Then they came to the general store.

There was a T-shirt and matching cap

in the window.

The T-shirt said

FAR OUT FRISBEES

on it in blue.

A sign said:

"Maybe you don't have to buy

more soap to make more money,"

said Violet.

"Maybe you have enough right now."

Arthur and Violet

went into the store.

"How much is the sample

in the window?" asked Arthur.

"$4.25," said the saleslady.

"Do you have enough money?"

"I don't know," said Arthur.

"I have to count it."

He poured his money out of the bag.

"It will take a long time

to count all that," said the lady.

"No it won't," said Violet.

"Arthur knows numbers,

and I have the numbers

written down."

She gave Arthur the paper
with the numbers on it.
"Let's see," said Arthur.
"$3.78, take away 53¢,
take away 27¢,
add 42¢,
add 34¢,
add 36¢,
add 33¢.
Hmmnnnn . . ."

"That's $4.43," said the lady.

"You have enough

for the T-shirt and cap,

and 18¢ left over."

"Wow!" said Arthur.

"I'll take the T-shirt and cap,

and do you have

any licorice twists?"

55

"Yes," said the lady.

"They are 5¢ apiece

or six for a quarter."

"How many do I get for 18¢?"

asked Arthur.

"You'll see," said the lady.

She winked at Violet.

Violet looked at Arthur.

"Arthur," she said,

"you said you knew numbers."

"Here are five licorice twists,"

said the lady.

"I've given you two extra

for good luck."

"Arthur," said Violet,

"if I have five peas

and you take three

and give me back two . . ."

"Wait," said Arthur.

"Change the peas to licorice twists,

and I will help you."

"Okay," said Violet.

"How many licorice twists
will I have?"

"Hold out your hand," said Arthur.

He gave Violet

the five licorice twists.

Then he took away three,

and gave back two.

"You would have
four licorice twists,"
said Arthur.
"But that only leaves me
with ONE!"

"You *do* know numbers, Arthur,"

said Violet,

and she started to eat

her licorice twists.

Arthur looked

at the one he had left.

"I got mixed up," he said.

"You would only have two."

"I know," said Violet.

"Because if you took

three licorice twists,

you wouldn't give back any!

You just love licorice twists!"

So Violet and Arthur

shared the licorice twists,

and they each had

two and a half!

E
HOB

Hoban, Lillian

Arthur's funny
money

$10.89

DATE			